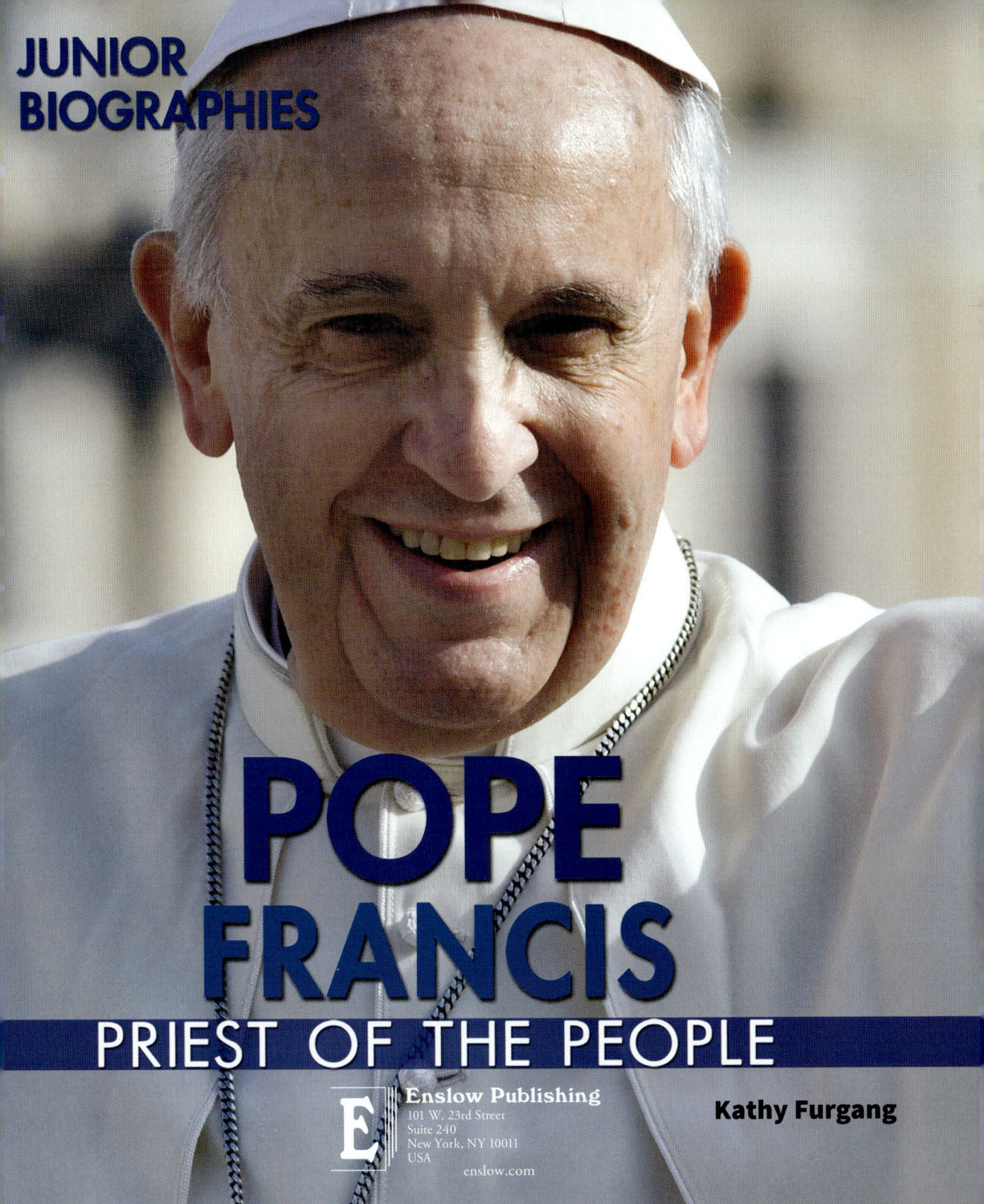

Words to Know

cardinal An important leader in the Catholic Church.

Catholic Church A world-wide Christian religion with over 1.2 billion members.

devoted Loving and loyal toward something.

elect To choose.

missionary A person sent on a religious mission, especially to help people in a foreign country.

poverty The state of being poor and not having enough money to live well.

priest A leader in the Catholic religion who oversees a church or group of followers.

religion A belief or system of worship of a god.

retire To leave a job and career, usually due to age.

Contents

Words to Know 2

Chapter 1 What Is a Pope? 5

Chapter 2 A Life in the Church 9

Chapter 3 Pope Francis 13

Chapter 4 A Pope of the People 18

Timeline 22

Learn More 23

Index 24

CHAPTER 1
What Is a Pope?

Did you know that there are thousands of **religions** throughout the world? A religion is a belief system that people follow. A religion can tell people how to live. It usually means believing in a power that controls our world, such as a god.

Although there are thousands of religions, there are a few main religions. The **Catholic Church** is one of those main religions. There are over a billion Catholic people around the world. The leader of that church is called the pope. There have been 266 popes throughout the history of the church.

Pope Francis Says:

"Life is a journey. When we stop, things don't go right."

POPE FRANCIS: PRIEST OF THE PEOPLE

A crowd at the Vatican celebrates after Jorge Mario Bergoglio is elected as the new pope in 2013.

FINDING A POPE

When a pope **retires**, the leaders of the church choose a new one. In 2013, they **elected** a **priest** from Argentina named Jorge Mario Bergoglio. As the pope, Jorge would be the highest leader of the Catholic Church. He would live in an area inside Rome, Italy, called Vatican City. The Vatican is the center of the Catholic Church.

Pope Francis greets people after saying Mass at a Palm Sunday service in 2017.

POPE FRANCIS: PRIEST OF THE PEOPLE

Jorge Mario Bergoglio chose the name Francis after Saint Francis of Assisi. He died in 1226 in Italy, and had a love for animals and nature. He had a respect for those who lived a simple life, and he lived his own life in **poverty**.

A New Name

Now that Jorge was the church's highest leader, he had to choose a new name for himself. He chose to be named after an important person in the history of the church. Now people no longer call him Jorge. They call him Pope Francis.

Chapter 2
A Life in the Church

Jorge Mario Bergoglio was born on December 17, 1936, in Buenos Aires, Argentina. Both of his parents were Italian. Jorge was one of five children in his family. When he was young, he had a serious infection in his lungs. He had to have surgery to remove part of the lung.

Choosing His Path

When Jorge got older, he trained as a scientist. He studied chemistry and worked

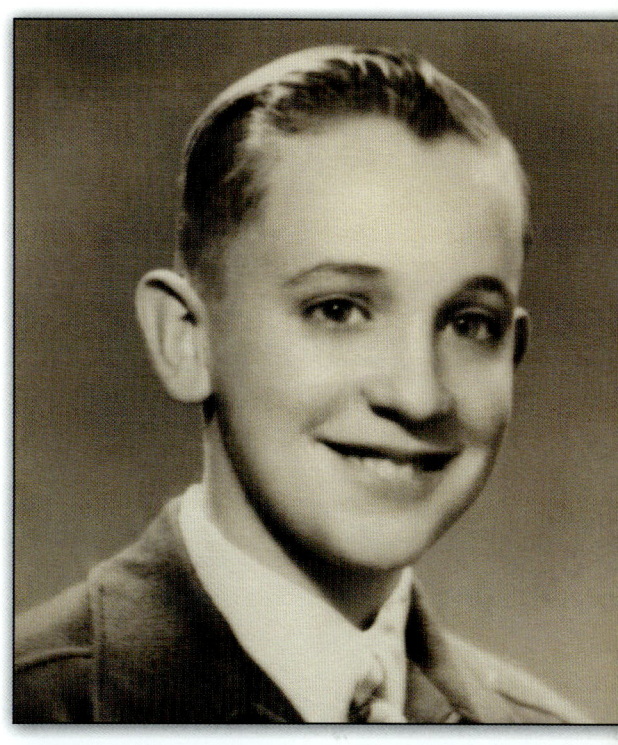

Jorge Mario Bergoglio as a child. He loved to play soccer when he was young, but he says he was not very good at it.

POPE FRANCIS: PRIEST OF THE PEOPLE

> **Pope Francis Says:**
> "Find new ways to spread the word of God to every corner of the world."

in a laboratory. He was also a teacher. But what he really wanted to do was to **devote** his life to God and the Catholic Church. In December 1969, Jorge became a priest.

A Jesuit Life

The type, or order, of priests that Jorge belonged to is called the Jesuits. They are known for doing **missionary** work. This is work done to help people in need. They help the poor around the world. Jorge felt that helping the poor was important. He has always felt that living like the poor could help people live a better life.

A Life in the Church

Jorge (*standing, second from left*) with his parents, brothers, and sisters. He was a new priest at this time.

Pope Francis: Priest of the People

When Jorge was a cardinal, he could have lived in a fancy apartment that was paid for by the church. Instead, he lived in his own small apartment. He cooked his own meals. He took a bus to work. He felt it was important to live a simple life.

Jorge worked for years as a priest in Buenos Aires. He rose to become a leader of the church. He even reached the highest level of priests before the pope, called a **cardinal**. Jorge became one of the most respected leaders of the Catholic Church.

Chapter 3
Pope Francis

In 2013, Pope Benedict XVI decided to retire. That meant that the Catholic Church needed to choose a new pope. A group of leaders met and went through the special process together. After talking and voting, they chose Jorge.

There were many "firsts" by picking Jorge. He was the first pope from modern times who was not from Europe. Even though his parents were from Italy, Jorge had been born and raised in Latin America. He was a leader of the church in that part of the world. He was also the first Jesuit pope. Jesuits are known for teaching people and for helping those in need. He was even the first to choose the name Francis.

Pope Francis Says:
"It seems to me that my brother cardinals have chosen one who is from faraway … Here I am. I would like to thank you for your embrace."

Pope Francis at his inauguration on March 19, 2013.

MAKING A DIFFERENCE

From his earliest days as leader, Pope Francis was different from the popes who came before him. When he moved to Vatican City to live, he returned to pay the last bill for the apartment he was leaving. He could have sent a servant instead of returning in person. He also chose to live in a home that was not built for the pope.

When the pope meets with leaders and makes speeches, he also meets with the poor. He washes the feet of the poor. This shows his devotion to helping them. He visits people in prison, too. He wants people to know that the church has not forgotten them. He wants to set an example to show people that everyone is a "child of God."

> Pope Francis speaks three languages—Spanish, Italian, and German—and understands many others, such as English, French, and Portuguese.

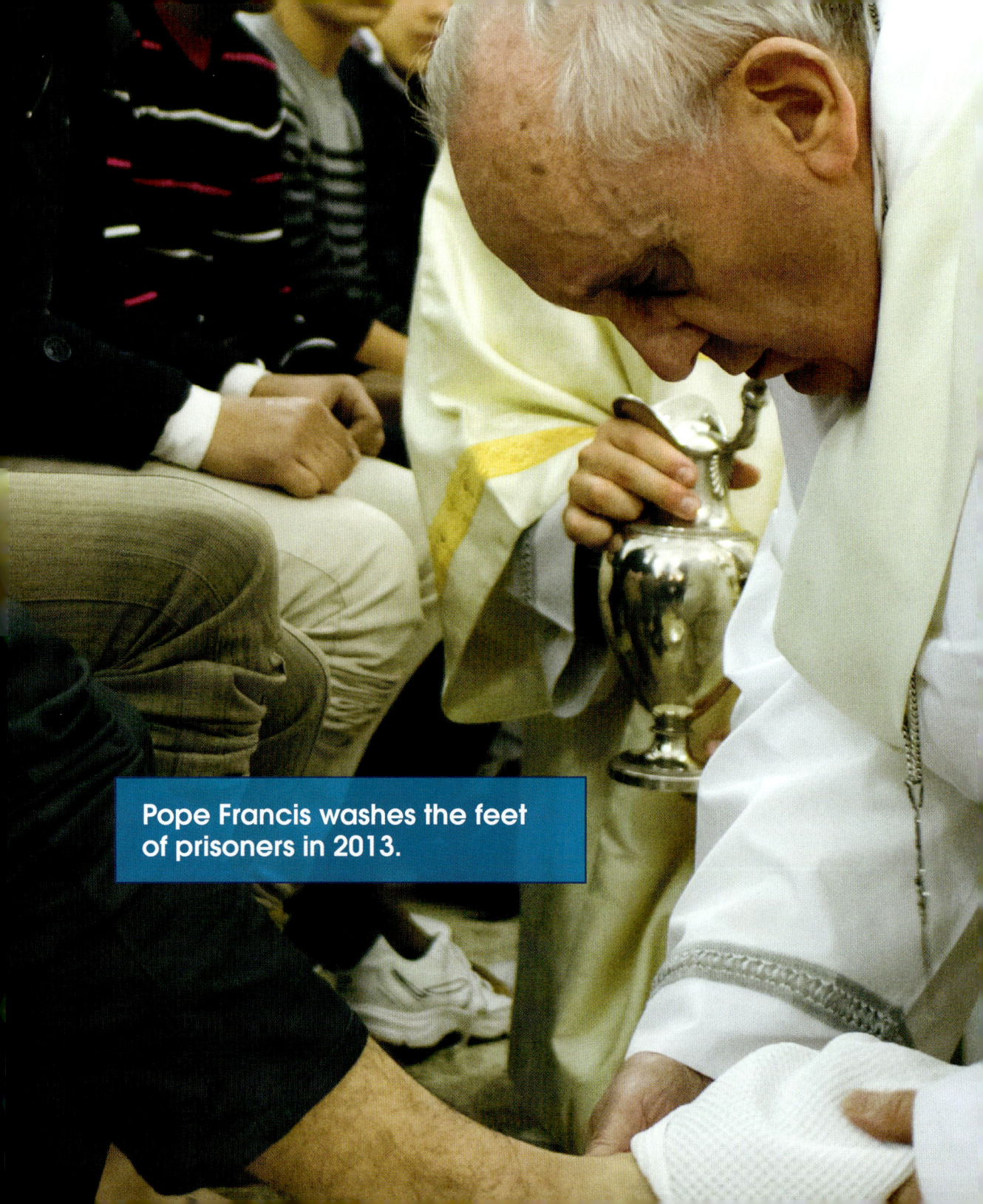

Pope Francis washes the feet of prisoners in 2013.

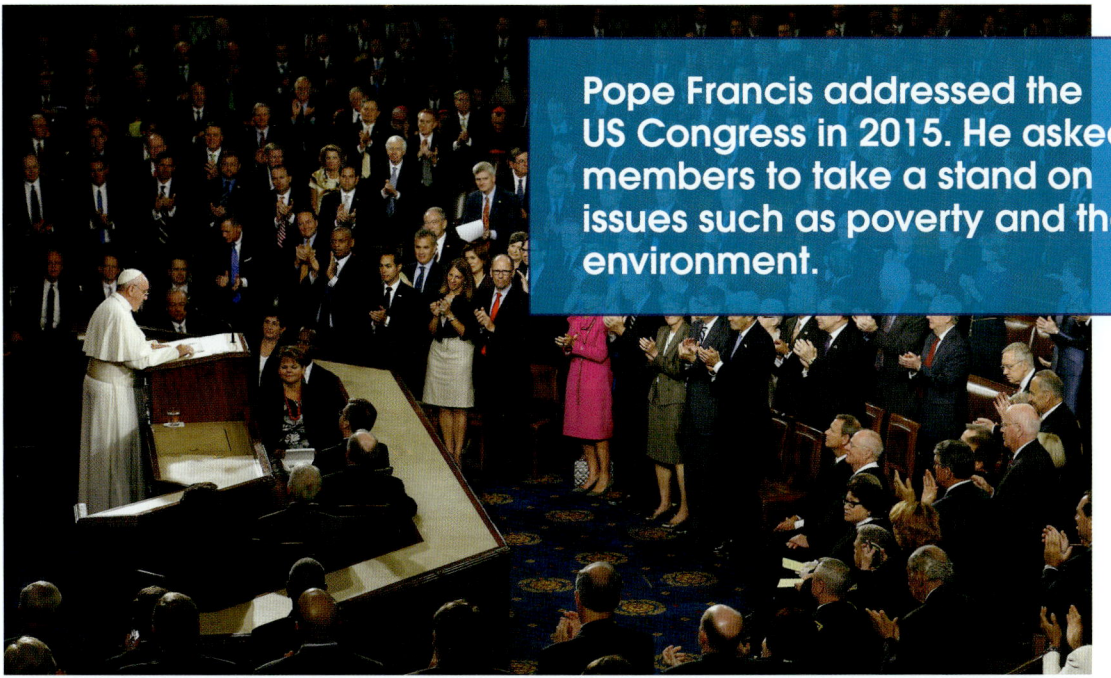

Pope Francis addressed the US Congress in 2015. He asked members to take a stand on issues such as poverty and the environment.

Speaking His Mind

Not all popes get involved in the news of the world. Pope Francis is not afraid to tell people what he thinks is fair and unfair. He has spoken to leaders of countries around the globe. He has encouraged nations around the world to help the poor, even if they are not countries with many Catholic people. He has spoken out against governments that encourage some to get rich while most people remain poor. He has spoken out against laws and ideas that do not consider the rights of average people.

Chapter 4
A Pope of the People

There are traditions that most popes follow. One is to stand on a platform when he is introduced to the world as the new pope. This places him above the other cardinals around him. It is a reminder of the pope's power over the church. Pope Francis does not stand above others to show his high position. He wants to meet everyone on the same level.

Role Model

Pope Francis is sometimes called the "pope of the people." He lives his daily life as a model for the way he hopes others will live their lives. He lives a simple life. He shows kindness instead of judgment.

> To mark his seventy-eighth birthday, Pope Francis donated four hundred sleeping bags to the homeless in Rome.

> Pope Francis stands with cardinals after his election. He chose to stand next to the cardinals and treat them as equals.

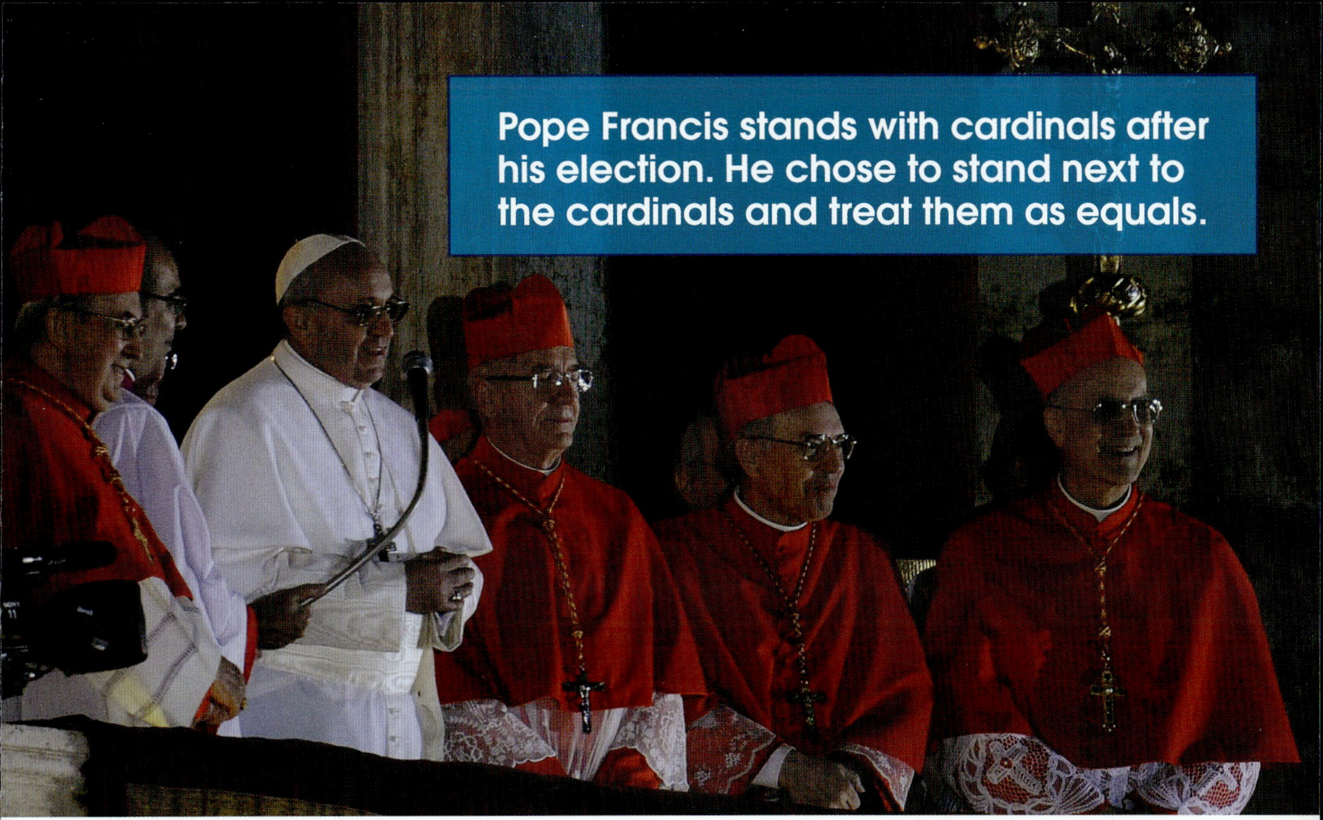

CHANGING THE CHURCH?

Many people wonder if having a leader like Pope Francis can help the church. Pope Francis has a Twitter account with more than 12 million followers. It is

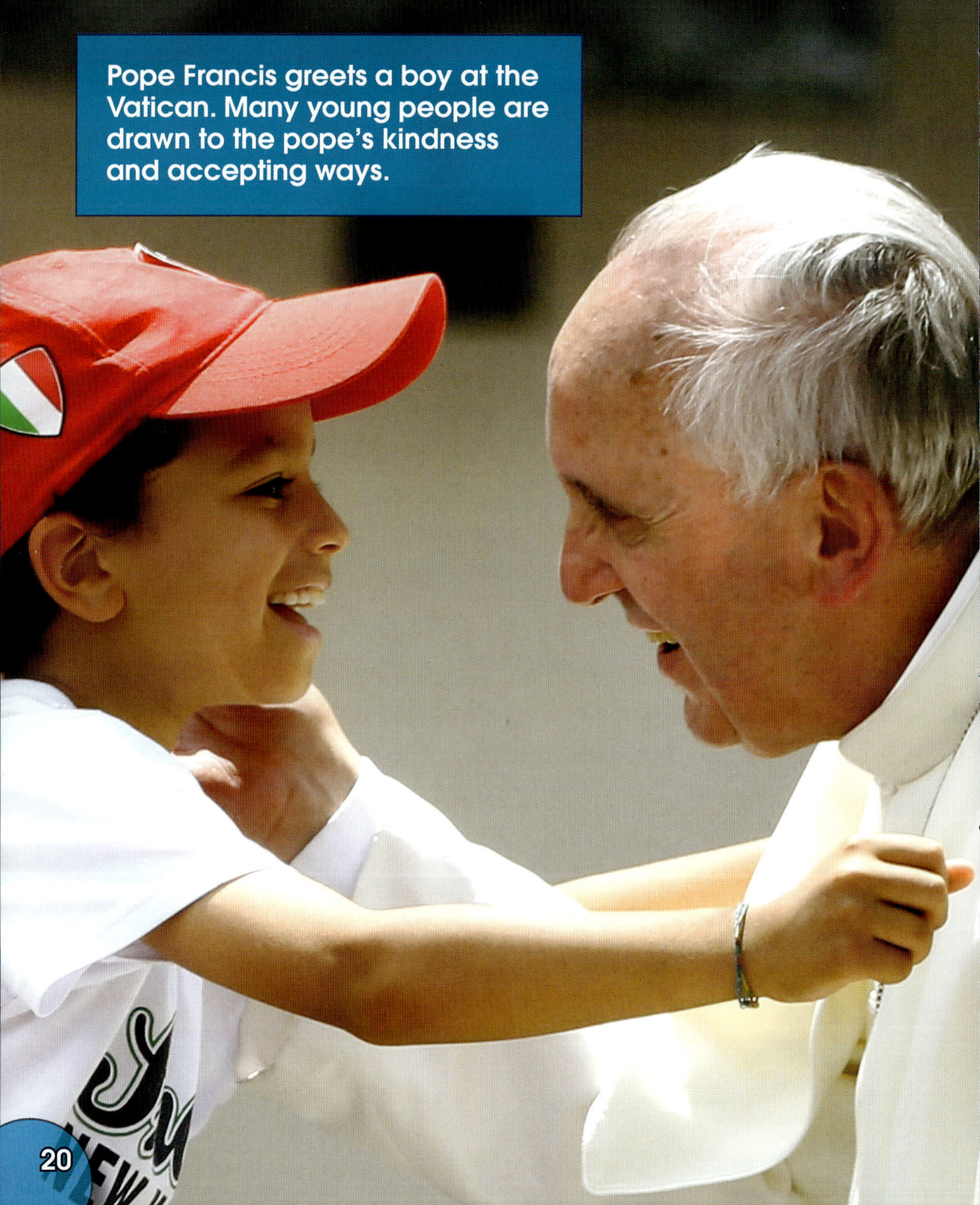

Pope Francis greets a boy at the Vatican. Many young people are drawn to the pope's kindness and accepting ways.

not just Catholics who follow his model of kindness. People around the world admire, or like, his ways. He is accepting of people and ideas that the church has not accepted before. He is open to new ideas and new rules for the church. This can bring new people to the church. It can keep the church strong for many years to come. It can also help the Catholic Church relate well to people of all faiths.

Pope Francis Says:
"We all have the duty to do good."

Timeline

1936 Jorge Mario Bergoglio is born in Buenos Aires.

1958 Earns a diploma as a chemical technician.

1966 Teaches high school in Buenos Aires.

1969 Becomes a priest.

1998 Is named archbishop of Buenos Aires.

2001 Is chosen by Pope John Paul II to become a cardinal.

2013 Is elected pope; chooses the name Francis.

2015 Makes first trip to United States; speaks to Congress.

Learn More

Books
Francis, Pope. *Dear Pope Francis: The Pope Answers Letters from Children Around the World.* Chicago, IL: Loyola Press, 2016.

Kramer, Barbara. *National Geographic Readers: Pope Francis.* Washington, DC: National Geographic Children's Books, 2015.

Monette, John. *Francis, the Pope for Kids.* Liguori, MO: Liguori Publications, 2015.

Websites
The Holy See
w2.vatican.va/content/vatican/en.html
Visit the Vatican's official website for Pope Francis for photos, videos, a biography, and news.

Pope Francis Twitter Page
twitter.com/Pontifex?ref_src=twsrc%5Egoogle%7Ctwcamp%5Eserp%7Ctwgr%5Eauthor
Check out the Pope's Twitter page to read his latest words of encouragement to his followers.

Index

B
Benedict XVI (pope), 13
Buenos Aires, Argentina, 6, 9, 12

C
cardinals, 12, 13, 18
Catholic Church, 5, 6, 10, 12, 13, 21

E
early priesthood, 10, 12
election as pope, 6, 13

H
helping the poor, 10, 15, 17

J
Jesuits, 10, 13

N
name choice, 8, 13

S
scientist and teacher, 9–10
simple way of living, 8, 12, 18

T
Twitter, 19

V
Vatican City, 6, 15

W
world governments, 17

Published in 2018 by Enslow Publishing, LLC.
101 W. 23rd Street, Suite 240, New York, NY 10011

Copyright © 2018 by Enslow Publishing, LLC.
All rights reserved.

No part of this book may be reproduced by any means without the written permission of the publisher.

Library of Congress Cataloging-in-Publication Data
Names: Furgang, Kathy, author.
Title: Pope Francis : priest of the people / Kathy Furgang.
Description: New York : Enslow Publishing, 2018. | Series: Junior biographies| Includes bibliographical references and index. | Audience: Grades 3-5
Identifiers: LCCN 2017020070| ISBN 9780766090514 (library bound) | ISBN 9780766090491 (pbk.) | ISBN 9780766090507 (6 pack)
Subjects: LCSH: Francis, Pope, 1936–Juvenile literature. |Popes–Biography–Juvenile literature.
Classification: LCC BX1378.7 .F87 2017 | DDC 282.092 [B] –dc23
LC record available at https://lccn.loc.gov/2017020070

Printed in China

To Our Readers: We have done our best to make sure all website addresses in this book were active and appropriate when we went to press. However, the author and the publisher have no control over and assume no liability for the material available on those websites or on any websites they may link to. Any comments or suggestions can be sent by email to customerservice@enslow.com.

Photo Credits: Cover, p. 1 Martin Podzorny/Shutterstock.com; pp. 2, 3, 22, 23, 24, back cover (curves graphic) Alena Kazlouskaya/Shutterstock.com; pp. 4, 9, 20 Franco Origlia/Getty Images; p. 6 Johannes Eisele/AFP/Getty Images; p. 7 NurPhoto/Getty Images; p. 11 API/Gamma-Rapho/Getty Images; p. 14 © AP Images; p. 16 Vandeville Eric/ABACA/Newscom; p. 17 Win McNamee/Getty Images; p. 19 Ettore Ferrari/EPA/Newscom; interior page bottoms (cross and lily) OlgaChernyak/Shutterstock.com.